Bernadette Watts, known throughout Europe simply as Bernadette, has illustrated many dozens of folk- and fairy tales. Born in England, she loved to draw from childhood. She studied at the Maidstone Art School in Kent, UK, and for some time was taught by Brian Wildsmith and David Hockney. Bernadette's many beautiful books include *The Snow Queen* and *The Little Drummer Boy*. Bernadette finds her inspiration in nature. Today she lives and works in Kent. She has been illustrating for NorthSouth Books and NordSüd Verlag since the beginning of her career fifty years ago.

First published in Switzerland under the title *Hans Millerman*.

First published in the United States, Great Britain, Canada, Australia, and New Zealand in 2022 by NorthSouth Books Inc., an imprint of NordSüd Verlag AG, CH-8005 Zürich, Switzerland.

Distributed in the United States by NorthSouth Books Inc.,
New York 10016.
Library of Congress Cataloging-in-Publication Data is available.

Printed in Latvia, by Livonia Print, Riga

ISBN: 978-0-7358-4489-6 (trade)
1 3 5 7 9 • 10 8 6 4 2
www.northsouth.com

Hans Millerman

Bernadette Watts

North
South

There once was a miller called Hans Millerman. He lived alone in his mill, for he had neither wife nor family. The great winds and the summer sun were his only companions.

In the autumn, the harvest having been gathered, Hans tilled his fields and sowed new corn.

"Ah," said Hans to himself when all the corn was sown, "how empty these fields look now. And how empty seems this life to me."

During the long winter days, the wind turned ceaselessly in the sails of the mill, creaked among the rafters, and swept under the door.

"Ah," said Hans to himself, "how lonely is the wind. And how lonely seems this life to me."

Then it was spring. Hans Millerman opened his door and saw the young leaves unfolding and the new corn pricking through the dark earth.

A bird was singing in a tree.

"Ah," said Hans to himself, "how solitary is that little bird. And how solitary seems this life to me."

The sun rose earlier every day. The earth became warm and strong. It was summer and the corn stood high.

The miller waited patiently for the harvest. By the door of the mill a red rose climbed with a white rose above the lintel, binding themselves together and around the windows.

"Ah," said Hans to himself, "how happy is the wild red rose when it loves the wild white rose. How happy I might be too had I a friend to love."

Early one morning Hans Millerman saw the corn was golden and ready to reap. So he went out to harvest. A great wind filled the sails of the mill.

The evening star was bright before the day's work was done. Then Hans returned to the mill. He looked out the window and made a wish on the harvest moon. "Before next full moon let me find a friend." Then he turned from the window, and as he did so he noticed a caterpillar sitting on the sill. The miller knocked the caterpillar onto the floor. The caterpillar crawled to the chair where Hans used to sit in the evenings. Hans, seeing the caterpillar had settled down, went to bed himself and slept soundly.

In the morning Hans dressed himself and saw that the caterpillar was sitting on his hat, just over the left eye.

"Well, I suppose you may as well sit there as anywhere," said Hans to the caterpillar. "At least you will be out of mischief." And he put on his hat and went out into the fields to work, and the caterpillar sat on the brim of the hat all day, until evening. And so it was the same every day. But Hans took no notice of the caterpillar at all. He neither talked to it by day nor offered it warmth by night.

The day came when all the crop was gathered and milled. Hans worked hard tying up the bags of flour, and while he was doing so the caterpillar fell off his hat onto the dusty floor.

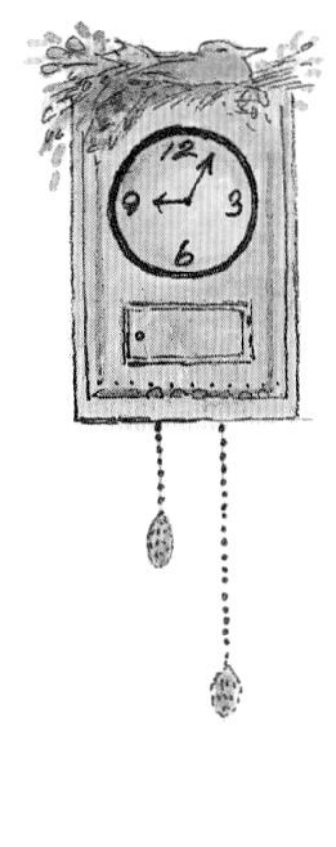

The miller was angry, and because he was tired, he spoke sharply to the caterpillar. "You really are a liability," he said. "Don't you think I have enough troubles without having to worry what you will do next. If you want to stay here you should do your share of the work."

The caterpillar, of course, was too small to help the miller with his work. . . . It could neither sow nor reap; nor could it help repair the mill during the long winter that was soon approaching. So it just went on sitting on Hans's hat by day and at night curled up on the windowsill or by the leg of Hans's chair.

The miller became angrier and angrier with the caterpillar. "I wish you would leave me alone," he said. "There is so much to do, and you are always getting in my way. How I wish I had a good friend to help a little." The caterpillar continued to sit on the miller's hat.

It was the time of the full moon again. The miller felt more lonely than ever. He gazed out his window and watched the moon rise amid the stars. "Well, moon," he said, "I asked you to grant me but a simple gift, and this you have not been able to do. Now I must try my luck for myself." So Hans Millerman packed a few things into a parcel, washed his face and hands, and put on his boots. He said to the caterpillar, "A man is lonely unless he has a friend to love—I must travel into the world to find a friend to love too. Now, get off my hat and on the floor where you belong. I am leaving this creaky old mill, but you might as well stay if you wish."

And so saying the miller left. He locked the door of the mill and hung the key on a nail. The caterpillar sadly watched Hans Millerman stride off into the night, and then it began to feel sleepy. It felt more and more sleepy, more than ever before.

And then the little caterpillar did fall asleep—but before it did so, it wove itself a furry blanket and wrapped itself up warmly because it felt so tired that it knew it would be asleep for a long, long time.

Meanwhile, Hans Millerman had travelled many miles into the world and dawn was breaking. It was midwinter. Snow fell peacefully and the whole world was white.

One snowflake fell on the miller's hand. "How pretty you are, little snowflake," said the miller. "I am a lonely man in this great strange world. Perhaps you could come along with me and be a friend to travel by my side."

But the snowflake was so frail that before she could answer she had melted quite away. Hans Millerman said to himself, “I must travel on farther, and in a little while I know I will meet a real friend.”

So he travelled on until it was spring. Then one night he lay down to rest under a hedge. When the sun rose the next morning, he saw on the road close by a little wild pansy, sometimes called the heart's-ease.

"How lovely and fresh you are, little flower," said the miller. "I am indeed a lonely traveler in this wide world. Perhaps you could come along with me and be a friend to travel by my side." But before the little flower could speak the heat of the sun had wilted her, and it was not long before she was quite dead.

Hans Millerman felt the ache of loneliness in his heart even more when the little flower was gone. But he said to himself, "I must travel on farther and in a little while perhaps I will meet a real friend."

So he travelled on until spring turned into summer. The days were very hot, and one evening the miller came to the bank of a cool stream where he could lie down to rest. The evening star rose as the sun set. The moon came out, and the night sky was littered with stars.

"Ah, little stars," said the miller, "how many friends you have up there. And here I am, with not even one." Just then a fox came by to drink at the cool stream. "How gentle you look, little fox," said the miller. "I am indeed a lonely man who can travel no farther through this wide world. But perhaps you could sit here and be a friend by my side." But before Hans had finished speaking, the fox had turned tail and disappeared into a field of high-grown corn. By the light of the moon, Hans Millerman could see that the field would soon be ready for reaping. And in his mind's eye he saw his own fields of corn, high and golden, waiting to be cut. But he said to himself, "Somehow I must travel on farther, even though I am so weary, and maybe someday I will meet a real friend."

Hans travelled slowly now, as summer turned into autumn. He came to wide open fields covered with wheat as far as the eye could see. Just then, a great wind came across the plain, and the wheat bowed before it in waves.

"How strong and great you are, wind," said the miller. "I am a lonely man, and I feel I have reached the end of the world, and there is no one here except you and me. Perhaps we could travel together at one another's side?"

The wind sighed. “I am the wild wind and can follow no other path but my own. I have work to do, and you, Hans Millerman, have work to do, too.” The sound of the wind reminded the miller of his home, and in his imagination he could hear the wind fill the sails of the mill. And there would be no one there to gather the harvest and grind the corn.

Hans hung his head in shame. It was late in the day; evening clouds fathered across the sky. Hans felt all his strength had gone, but he turned his face in the direction of his own land and began to travel back.

He walked without rest until he reached his fields. Dawn was breaking. The sun came up, and the wind ran down the hillside and filled the sails of the mill with a great sound.

Hans Millerman suddenly felt the ache lift from his heart, and he wondered if the little green caterpillar would be sitting on the windowsill when he entered the mill and whether it would sit on the brim of his hat as it did last year while he gathered the harvest and at night fall asleep by the leg of his chair.

He took the key from the nail and unlocked the door. But the caterpillar was not there. Nor was it sitting by the chair.

Then the heart of the miller was indeed heavy. "The caterpillar was a poor sort of friend," he said, "but it was better than no one."

Hans Millerman sighed, and as he did so he looked around at the familiar walls and objects that he had not seen for a whole year. He looked out at the golden corn, warm beneath the midday sun. He looked up at the huge beams above his head, and then he saw up there in the shadows a bright butterfly.

It was a very lovely butterfly, the loveliest butterfly Hans had ever seen. He did not want to frighten it away, so he stood quite still. Then the little butterfly fluttered down into the room; it came right over to the miller and settled on the brim of his hat, just above the left eye.

"Ah, little butterfly," said the miller, his heart full of happiness. "I have travelled right around the world in search of a friend to love. Had I but known that you were here I should have returned sooner. But there was only a caterpillar, and he, too, has gone now."

The butterfly spoke in a small voice. "The caterpillar came to be a friend to travel by your side. But the caterpillar was small and weak. And now the caterpillar has gone away and can never return."

"Never again will I drive away the offer of friendship. Not even from a caterpillar," Hans Millerman promised.

“I too am small and weak,” replied the butterfly, “but I am here to travel with you and be a friend by your side.”

So Hans Millerman went out to reap the corn that stood high and golden as far as the eye could see. And all the time that he worked the little butterfly sat on the

brim of his hat, just above the left eye. And at nightfall, when the miller went to bed tired, the butterfly folded its wings and slept by the leg of the miller's old chair.